Would you like FREE colo
for this book? Download tl

MW01090115

bookconnect.review/dp/worksheetsslowpokebusy

Check out more of Mother Melania's books at
amazon.com/author/mothermelania

bit.ly/Moses-Burning-Bush

*Old Testament Stories
for Children*

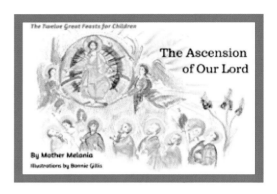

bit.ly/Ascension-Lord

*The Twelve Great
Feasts for Children*

bit.ly/Pascha-Feast

*The Three-Day Pascha: Orthodox
Christian Easter Stories for Children*

bit.ly/Scooter-Gets-Point

*The Adventures of
Kenny & Scooter*

PLEASE NOTE -Links are case sensitive

Slowpoke Sloth and Busy Beaver:
Easy Does It!

By Mother Melania

Illustrated by Cayce-Marie Halsell

Slowpoke Sloth lived at the Duck Pond. What on earth was a sloth doing so far away from his natural home?

Slowpoke had escaped while being moved to a new zoo. Well, he didn't exactly escape. His cage had bumped around and had become unlatched. Then the van ran out of gas, and the zookeeper walked off to find a gas station. Slowpoke didn't notice. He just stayed in the van and slept.

Eventually, Slowpoke got hungry. He bumped his
head against his cage door and it swung open.
Slowpoke slowly climbed out.

Nearby he spotted a tree, with tender leaves and
shoots to eat. In no real hurry, he climbed the tree.
After he'd munched some green shoots, he curled up
on a branch, and went back to sleep.

When the driver came back, he didn't notice that Slowpoke was gone. Later, Slowpoke woke up and found himself near the Duck Pond. There he lived from then on, in the same tree. Sloths, as you know, are in no special hurry to move.

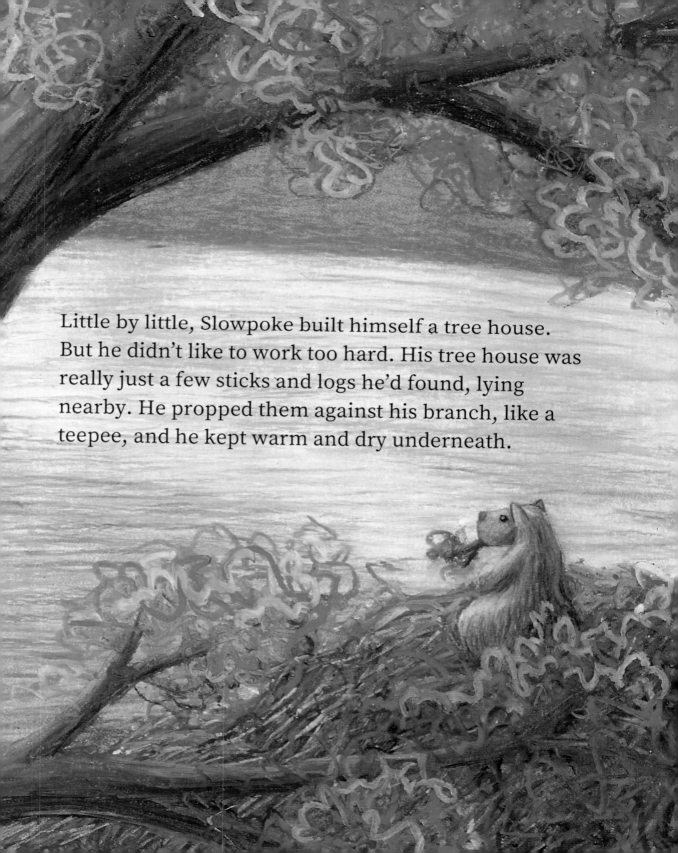

Little by little, Slowpoke built himself a tree house.
But he didn't like to work too hard. His tree house was
really just a few sticks and logs he'd found, lying
nearby. He propped them against his branch, like a
teepee, and he kept warm and dry underneath.

Slowpoke's tree was just downstream of Busy Beaver's dam. Busy didn't approve of Slowpoke's tree house at all.

"Slowpoke, that tree house is going to fall over in the first big storm," Busy said one day. "You need to make it strong. It should be attached to the tree."

Slowpoke considered these ideas. "Maybe. But … maybe later, Busy," he responded, with one eye closing.

"Slowpoke, you're the laziest animal I've ever met!" Busy replied.

Slowpoke looked down lazily from the branch where he was dozing, but he had no more to say.

"Did you hear me?" Busy asked. "Your tree house isn't safe. It needs more work."

Slowpoke nodded his head in reply. "Sometime soon, I'll fix it, Busy."

"I give up!" Busy said gruffly and went off in a huff to work on his dam.

Busy was very proud of his dam. When he was in a bad mood, he'd work on his dam. When he was sad, he'd work on his dam. When he was happy, he'd work on his dam. Beavers LOVE to work!

When Busy was tired, he'd rest in the warm, dry mound, up above the water inside his dam. Then he'd wake right up and start working some more.

Busy was an unusual beaver. Most beavers are concerned that their dams are built well, and built to last. Busy loved to work, work, work – but he didn't love to repair his dam.

Instead of finding weak spots, he was always making his dam higher, wider, and more beautiful. And the higher he made his dam, the more top heavy it became. Busy was too busy building to make repairs.

One day, Sage the Owl dropped in to visit Busy. Busy didn't have a high opinion of Sage. Sage spent a lot of time high in treetops looking out for danger below. To Busy, though, Sage just seemed to be wasting time.

"How are you, Busy?" asked Sage.

"Busy as a beaver, of course. Busy, busy, busy," replied Busy. "A dam takes lots and lots and lots of work. But I love it. It's very beautiful, don't you think?"

"Yes, it's certainly beautiful, but do you think a dam really needs to be so tall?"

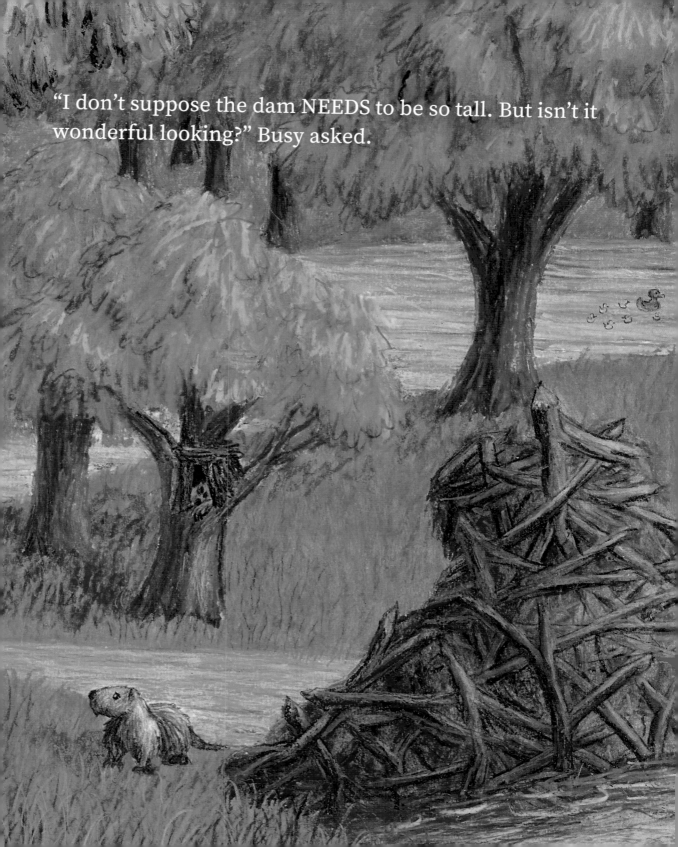

"I don't suppose the dam NEEDS to be so tall. But isn't it wonderful looking?" Busy asked.

Sage thought a bit. "I guess so, Busy. But you keep building higher and higher. I wonder if down below, at the base, it might need repairs by now?"

"I'll have plenty of time for repairs later. I'm building the most beautiful dam ever. Repairs can wait."

Sage shook his head. "I hope so, Busy," he said a little sadly. Then Sage flew away.

"What a busybody," grumbled the beaver. "He thinks he knows it all."

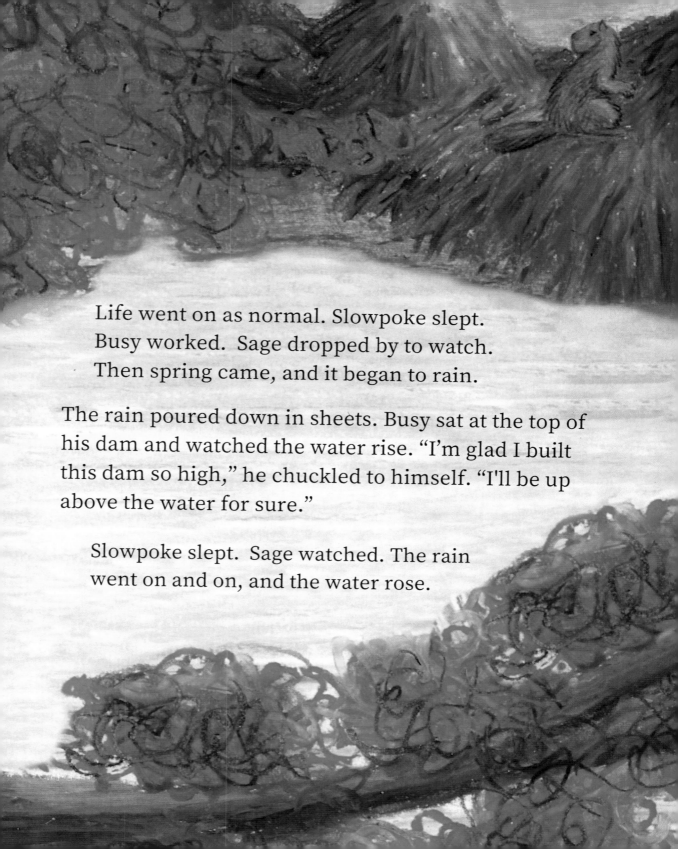

Life went on as normal. Slowpoke slept.
Busy worked. Sage dropped by to watch.
Then spring came, and it began to rain.

The rain poured down in sheets. Busy sat at the top of
his dam and watched the water rise. "I'm glad I built
this dam so high," he chuckled to himself. "I'll be up
above the water for sure."

Slowpoke slept. Sage watched. The rain
went on and on, and the water rose.

One day, Sage spotted a new leak in the dam. It was getting bigger by the minute. Sage hooted an alarm – just before the dam began to give way.

Busy heard Sage and leaped for the shore just before the entire dam collapsed. Crash went the dam, in a bundle of sticks and logs.

Downstream of the dam, Slowpoke was snoozing in his tree, when a rush of water shook him awake. Down Slowpoke fell, and down fell all the sticks and logs for his tree house.

Fearless knew that when Sage hooted, he had better come quickly. Fearless arrived just in time to fish Slowpoke out of the creek. Busy and Sage were waiting on the side of the creek.

Slowpoke looked sadly at his tree, surrounded by water now. All the pieces of his tree house were floating away

Slowpoke turned to Busy. "Maybe you WERE right, Busy," Slowpoke admitted. "Maybe I DID need a stronger tree house."

"I'll help you build it again," Busy said kindly. "We'll build it strong this time."

Then Busy turned to Sage. "And YOU were right too, Sage. I'll go right back to work on a new dam. And this time, I'll make SURE to keep up with repairs."

Sage, wise owl that he was, didn't say anything. He just nodded.

Slowpoke Sloth and Busy Beaver: Easy Does It!

from *Fearless and Friends*

Story © copyright 2010 by Mother Melania
Illustrations © copyright 2010 by Cayce-Marie Halsell

All rights reserved.

Published by Holy Assumption Monastery
1519 Washington St.
Calistoga, CA 94515

Phone: (707) 942-6244
Website: https://holyassumptionmonastery.com
Email: sisters@holyassumptionmonastery.com

If you liked this book, please consider
purchasing some of the other books in the series

bit.ly/Capers-Harry

bit.ly/Greedy-Crow

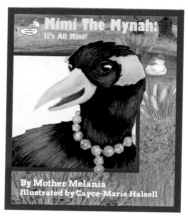

bit.ly/Mimi-Mynah

And please check out our monastery's line of journals at
amazon.com/author/holyassumptionmonastery

bit.ly/Every-Thanks

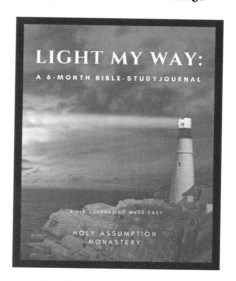

bit.ly/Light-My-Way

PLEASE NOTE -Links are case sensitive

Please leave a review of this book on Amazon at

amzn.to/3Q1BZpy

We're always looking for feedback and ways to improve!

Thanks so much, and God bless you!

ABOUT THE AUTHOR AND ILLUSTRATOR

Mother Melania is the abbess of Holy Assumption Monastery in Calistoga, California. She has enjoyed working with children all of her life. In addition to The Three-Day Pascha series, she has written several other series of children's books, focusing on Scriptural stories and Great Feasts of the Church, and celebrating the virtues.

Cayce-Marie Halsell is an Orthodox Christian iconographer and illustrator. She lives in Santa Barbara, California with her family. You can see more of her work at www.cmhicons.weebly.com